THE GIFT OF THE MAGIC

and other enchanting character-building stories for smart teenage girls who want to grow up to be strong women

by

Richard Showstack

Illustrated by Eric Whitfield

BeachHouse Books
Chesterfield Missouri, USA

Copyright

Graphics Credits:

Cover by Dr. Bud Banis. based on drawings by Eric Whitfield with text
and enhancements by Dr. Banis. Photograph of Richard Showstack by Jun
Yokota

Publication date July, 2004

ISBN 1-888725-64-8 Regular print BeachHouse Books Edition

First Printing, July, 2004

Library of Congress Cataloging-in-Publication Data

BeachHouse
Books

an Imprint of

Science & Humanities Press

PO Box 7151

Chesterfield, MO 63006

(636) 394-4950

To my father

Dr. Nathaniel Showstack

who supported me

in more ways than one.

Acknowledgments

Thanks to Donie Nelson, Patt Healy and J. T. O'Hara for their continuing support and encouragement.

Thanks to Dr. Laura Schlessinger for her inspiration.

Thanks to Dennis Prager and Larry Elder for making me think.

Thanks to Dr. Bud Banis for believing in me (and my writing).

And a special thanks to my wonderful and talented illustrator, Eric Whitfield, who (almost) never got mad as I asked him time and again to do new versions of his illustrations until they matched my vision of them.

Contents

Many young people want to become doctors or lawyers because of the money and prestige that go along with those professions.

But a lucky few discover at an early age what they were put on this earth to do...

The Gift of the Magic

Despite the fact that she was about to graduate from high school and had her whole life ahead of her, Tanya was bored. She had gotten good grades in high school due to sheer will power, and had been accepted at a prestigious college, but now she really couldn't care less about anything they were teaching her in school.

All she wanted to do was draw, and she was good at it. But she figured nobody would pay her to draw pictures, so she might as well get a college degree and become a lawyer or businesswoman or something.

Then one day while shopping on Main Street with her mother, Tanya saw an old woman selling the most unusual pottery she had ever seen. The pottery had, well, the only word that Tanya could think of to describe what it had was "emotion," as if the person who had created it had left a little bit of himself in it. Just looking at it started to create certain feelings inside of Tanya...

Tanya wanted to stop and examine the pottery, but her mother told her it was not a good idea to talk to "street people," so they kept on walking.

The next time Tanya was walking by herself on Main Street, however, she looked for the old woman, and, when she couldn't find her, she asked some of the other street merchants if they knew where she might be found.

"Oh, you mean Mabel Jackson," replied one of them. "Crazy as a loon. Says she hears voices. I think she has a studio over on Second Street."

So, despite her fear of being in that part of the city alone, Tanya walked over to Second Street. Then she walked up and down the street, looking into every window she passed.

And sure enough, after walking just a couple blocks, Tanya saw Mabel Jackson through a window, smoking a cigar and sitting at her pottery wheel, working on a pot. She was wearing the same bandanna and clay-splattered long-sleeve shirt over a tee-shirt that she had on the week before on Main Street.

After a minute, Mabel noticed the young woman staring in the window and motioned for her to come in. So Tanya went in and sat down on a bench in front of Mabel's work area.

"I'm sorry to bother you, Mrs. Jackson," explained Tanya. "But last week I saw you on Main Street and I thought your work was the most unusual pottery I'd ever seen. I'd never seen anything like it."

"Well, thank you, young lady. And please call me 'Mabel'."

"Thank you, 'Mabel'. My name is Tanya."

"Are you an artist, Tanya?"

"Well, no," Tanya said blushing. "At least not a very good one," she lied. "I do like to draw a little, but it's just a hobby."

"Well how's about you showing me some of your work, sometime, Tanya? I always like to see the work of young artists."

Nobody had ever called her drawings "her work" before, nor had anyone ever referred to her as an "artist."

"Well, I guess I could, the next time I'm in the neighborhood, I mean."

"Sure, any time," said Mabel. "You can always find me, either here in my studio or selling my stuff over on Main Street."

And with that, Tanya got up to leave.

But Mabel called her back. "Here, why don't you take this pot," she said, handing Tanya the most beautiful vase she had ever seen.

"Oh, no, I could never afford to pay you for this."

"Don't worry. It's a gift from God," said Mabel, smiling and waving Tanya away with her hand. Then Mabel looked down and went back to her work.

Tanya felt wonderful after she left! Nobody had ever paid any serious attention to her drawing before. And she couldn't believe how generous Mabel had been in giving her such a beautiful vase.

And when she got home, Tanya started to look through her drawings to pick out the best ones to show Mrs. Jackson, uh, I mean, Mabel.

The next time Tanya had a free afternoon, she gathered up her drawings and headed downtown to see Mabel again. She couldn't find her on Main Street, so Tanya headed over to Second Street to see if Mabel was in her studio.

And, sure enough, there she was, working on a pot with a cigar in her mouth, a bandanna over her hair, and clay splattered everywhere.

Tanya knocked, and, without even looking up from what she was doing, Mabel motioned for her to come in. Then she motioned for Tanya to sit down, and Tanya understood that Mabel was deep in concentration and didn't want to be disturbed, so she sat and watched as Mabel worked on the pot.

It seemed like a miracle how, with the slightest movement of her hands or fingers, Mabel could alter the shape of the spinning pot. She was so deep in concentration that she seemed to be in a trance, relying on her sense of touch alone to shape the pot.

Finally, after about 15 minutes, Mabel stopped. She opened her eyes, looked at the pot for a moment, and then crushed it back into a pile of clay with her hands.

Tanya was shocked to see her destroy so easily something that she had been working on for so long.

"Nope, don't have it today," said Mabel, shaking her head.

"Don't have what?" asked Tanya.

"The magic," responded Mabel matter-of-factly.

Then Mabel stood up, dried her hands on a towel that looked like it had never been washed, and walked over to Tanya.

"You're the girl who was here last week, arncha?" she said, sitting down wearily next to Tanya. "Whaddya got there?"

"Oh, these are some of my drawings," answered Tanya. "Remember? You asked me to show them to you the next time I was in the neighborhood."

"Oh, yeah, now I remember," said Mabel, now wiping her forehead with a dirty handkerchief. "Let me see whacha got." And with that, she took Tanya's pictures and placed them on her lap.

Mabel looked carefully through Tanya's "portfolio," examining every picture carefully.

Finally, when she was apparently satisfied that she had seen what she had been looking for, she handed the pictures back to Tanya and said as she slowly stood up, "Yup, you got it!"

"Got what?" asked Tanya.

"The gift," replied Mabel. "The gift of the magic."

"The gift of the magic? What do you mean by that?" asked Tanya.

"The creative gift," explained Mabel, turning back toward Tanya, "the ability to make something appear that has never existed before anywhere in the universe except in our forgotten dreams. Some people got the gift of gab, some got green thumbs, some got the Midas touch, and some people got a science bug up their butts."

Tanya blushed.

"And some people, like you and me, we got the gift of the magic."

While Tanya pondered this, Mabel walked heavily over to a table, poured herself a cup of coffee, and asked if Tanya would like one.

Tanya rarely drank coffee, and she wondered how clean a coffee cup could be in a place like this, so she politely declined.

"How do you know I have 'the gift'?" asked Tanya.

"I just know," answered Mabel, putting down the coffee cup. "I been around art and artists long enough to know. In fact, I could tell the first time I saw you that you had it."

Tanya looked down at herself, wondering what it was that Mabel had seen that first time that had convinced her.

Mabel walked over to Tanya.

"Let me ask you this," said Mabel. "Do you sometimes have the feeling that you're just so full of ideas and images that if you don't put something down on paper that you'll explode?"

"Yes."

"And do you sometimes have the feeling that the picture you're going to draw already exists somewhere, and all you're doing is giving physical form to it?"

"Yes."

"And when you get into your art work, do you lose track of time and where you are? Do you sometimes have the feeling that you are no longer in control of your own hand, that the energy is just flowing through you, that you are merely the conduit for some higher creative force in the universe?"

"Yes! How did you know? That's exactly how it is!"

"And when you're drawing something, what gives you the most pleasure, doing the drawing itself or finishing it?"

Tanya had to think about that one. "Why, doing the drawing."

"And when you finally finish a drawing and look at what you've created, do you first feel an almost indescribable excitement, and then feel an almost indescribable sadness because what you have created isn't as perfect as the perfect image that you had in your mind?"

"Why, come to think of it, whenever I finish a drawing, I do feel that way. So then I immediately start thinking about what I can draw next."

"Hah!" cried out Mabel, making a sound like thunder as she clapped her hands together. "That proves it! You got the gift!"

Both of them were silent for a moment. Then Mabel spoke first.

"So you going to art school?" Mabel asked as she started to prepare another piece of clay.

"Oh, no," smiled Tanya. "I'm just a high school senior, and next year I'm going to college."

Hearing this, Mabel began to shake her head back and forth.

"What's wrong?" asked Tanya.

"Waste of time," said Mabel as she pounded her fists into the clay.

"Why do you say that?"

"Cuz it's true." Mabel looked up from the clay and at Tanya. "Look, not many people got the gift of magic. But once you got it, you can't get rid of it. It'll be with you all of your life, like someone constantly looking over your shoulder.

"You can pretend it's not there, you can try to do something else for a while, but then it won't let you concentrate on anything else. The best thing you can do is invite it to come sit down beside you so it can help you make whatever it is you were meant to make."

"Oh, but my parents..." began Tanya, but before she could finish, Mabel interrupted her.

"It don't matter what your parents or anyone else thinks!" she said, glaring at Tanya. "Look, God gave you the gift. He doesn't give it to every Tom or Dick or Harry down the street, you know.

"And if He gave it to you, he must have had a reason to, 'cuz He don't do nothin' without a reason, right? And if He gave it to you for a reason, then you got a responsibility not only to Him but to the whole world to share that gift with other people."

"But how can I make a living by drawing?" protested Tanya.

"Look," said Mabel, sitting herself down beside Tanya and taking Tanya's smooth clean hands into her own dirty callused ones. "Not everyone is made to be a lawyer or doctor or whatever. Some people got to be cooks or garbage collectors or sailors. And some people just got to be artists — that's just the way it is.

"And some people know from the start what they want to be for the rest of their lives, and others have to be led there, one step at a time.

"You don't know what God has in store for you. Maybe he wants you to be an artist for ten years and then become a lawyer.

"You just gotta believe that God knows what He's doin'."

Tanya still wasn't sure.

Mabel stood up, started to pace back and forth, and seemed to be trying to think of some other way to get across to Tanya what she meant.

"Listen, God's been practicin' this whole show for a long time, hasn't He? So don't you think that by now He's got it all figured out? Don't you think He's figured out how many accountants and cooks and baseball players and politicians we need in order to get by? And how many artists?

"He knows that people need to see and think about more than just what exists. So He gives some people the gift of the magic so they can draw or sculpt or build what they see in their dreams. And He's the one who puts it into their dreams in the first place!

"People who have the gift of magic shouldn't worry about sellin' their stuff or making money or getting married or how they dress or any of that stuff. God will take care of all that. They just gotta concentrate on giving form to what God whispers in their ears, whether it's about art or poetry or music or architecture, or whatever.

"People with the gift of the magic have been specially chosen, like saints. They're holy people!"

Tanya still wasn't sure what to think about all this, and Mabel seemed to be ready to start on another pot. So Tanya stood and explained that she had to be going.

By this time Mabel had already started working, lost in a trance with her eyes half closed, so she barely nodded when Tanya left.

In the Fall, Tanya entered the prestigious college that she had been accepted to. But she flunked out after only one year.

When her parents asked her why she couldn't seem to concentrate on her studies, Tanya didn't offer any explanation except to say something about the fact that it was hard to study with one person constantly whispering in your ear and another person looking over your shoulder all the time.

And the next year, Tanya enrolled in art school.

These days, people seem to think that they can buy a book, a videotape, or a course that will teach them the "secret of success." But maybe the "secret" is something we have to discover within ourselves...

The Man on the Hill

Jenny Jump-Up was bored. She couldn't think of anything interesting to do that afternoon.

She also couldn't decide what to do with the rest of her life.

Jenny lived in the village of Wallaroo in the Far District near the Eastern Sea. It was a prosperous village where everyone seemed to work hard and be happy with what they did.

But Jenny was fifteen years old, and in the village it was the tradition that young men and women should at least start working toward their goals when they became 16. (It was a very modern and politically correct place!)

Jenny had always wanted to be an engineer, designing bridges, battering rams, catapults, and so on. She also knew that not only was it hard to get into engineering school, but it was harder still to graduate and would take more than five years to do so. That was equal to a full third of the time she had already been alive. She would be twenty-two by the time she finished!

So Jenny went to her mother, who was a doctor, and asked her for advice about what to do with her life.

Now, her mother was a very wise woman (as mothers always are in stories like this), and she knew that directly giving her daughter advice would be useless — her daughter would just ignore it and go back to moping about how empty her life was.

So her mother simply told her, "If you need help deciding what to do with your life, you should go ask the Man on the Hill."

"Who?" asked Jenny.

"Why, the Man on the Hill," replied her mother. "When I was your age, I asked my mother the same question, and she gave me the same answer. After I went to see the Man on the Hill, I knew what I wanted to do with my life, and that was to become a doctor."

Well, hearing this, Jenny really thought her mother had gone off the deep end, so she let the subject drop. Besides, she didn't feel like wasting an afternoon looking for some strange old man who lived in the hills.

But the next time she was near the Wallaroo Elementary School, she decided to stop in and visit Mr. Bramblebush. Everyone at the school liked Mr. Bramblebush (although some children joked that he resembled a tumbleweed more than a bramble bush because he was so round that he looked like he would just keep rolling if someone gave him a shove).

As a young man, Mr. Bramblebush had worked as a banker but had decided to give up that line of work and become a school teacher instead. He had been Jenny's sixth grade teacher, and a very good one, too.

While visiting Mr. B. (as everyone referred to him), Jenny thought of the conversation she had had with her mother, and decided to ask Mr. Bramblebush for his advice.

"Mr. Bramblebush, what made you decide to give up your job as a banker and become an elementary school teacher?"

"That's easy to answer. I was at a point in my life when I wasn't happy and wasn't sure what to do next, so I decided to go see the Man on the Hill, and after I visited him

I knew what I wanted to do, which was to teach elementary school students."

Hearing this, Jenny's eyes opened as big as saucers! She couldn't believe what she had just heard!

Had both her mother and Mr. Bramblebush gone crazy? Or was there something to this Man on the Hill story after all?

"Mr. Bramblebush, this Man on the Hill guy must be pretty wise. Does he give the same advice to everyone?"

"Yes, I believe he does," Mr. B. answered.

"Well, then," continued Jenny, "why don't you just tell me his secret, and save me the trouble of going to see him?"

"Oh, I don't think I can do that," Mr. B. laughed. "Well, of course I could, but I don't think the Man on the Hill would like it at all if I did. I'm afraid you'll just have to go talk to him yourself."

By now, Jenny's curiosity had finally overcome her laziness, so she made up her mind to go talk to this "Man on the Hill," after all.

When she asked her mother for directions, her mother told her that if she just started to walk toward the hill, a path would appear to her, and that she should just follow that path until she found the Man on the Hill or he found her. Also, she told Jenny to make sure she went alone, because the Man on the Hill would not speak to her if she went with anyone else.

She also told Jenny that it was a long walk, so she should expect to spend the night on the hill. Last, she told Jenny that it would be a good idea to wait until the next full moon, for there were tales told of strange occurrences on the hill at night time.

The hill didn't look that big to Jenny, so, when the next full moon came around, she packed a lunch and started off (after telling her mother where she was going, of course).

But the closer she got to the hill, the bigger it seemed. In fact, when she had reached its base, it seemed more like a mountain than a hill!

For a moment she considered turning back, but she decided she had come this far so she might as well continue for a while.

And sure enough, after a while a path appeared out of the brush with a sign beside it that read: "Follow this path to the Man on the Hill."

This discovery made Jenny more excited than she could remember being for a long time, so she started to practically skip up the hill.

After climbing a long time, however, she started to get really tired and discouraged again. But just as she was once again considering turning back, she saw another sign that read: "Not much farther now. Don't give up!"

So, although it was getting dark and the weather looked threatening, Jenny kept on, vowing not to give up until she had reached her goal.

Finally she reached the top of the hill!

And there, in the middle of a clearing, she saw a big rock.

And there was something written on the rock in small letters.

Jenny could hardly contain her excitement, and she ran up to the rock as fast as she could on her weary legs.

This was the note on the rock: "I've decided to wait for you at the top of the next hill."

It was signed, "The Man on the Hill."

Well, this was discouraging news! But it was too late to go back down the hill, and besides, she was too tired to do so, so Jenny decided to spend the night there, just as her mother had foreseen, and return to Wallaroo the next morning.

That night was a terrible night! The wind roared and howled and the shadows from the full moon seemed like wild animals circling Jenny, getting ready to devour her!

And, although Jenny did not know it at the time, a pair of eyes were watching her all night long...

But somehow Jenny got through the night, and when she awoke the next morning, she had a new determination to find this Man on the Hill.

"The nerve of him changing which hill he was on without even telling anyone in the village below!" she thought.

"But I'm not turning back now, after all I've been through already!" she said, pulling herself up to her full height of four feet eleven inches. "I'll tell him!"

So Jenny headed off resolutely toward the top of the next hill, eating berries and whatever other wild fruits she could find for her breakfast.

Jenny finally got to a clearing on the next hill around noon. There she saw another large rock, which was shaped, in a strange way, like a man's head. This rock had a lot written on it in small letters.

As she approached the rock, she was as mad as, well, you know, and she vowed that no matter what this message said, she was not going to leave the hills until she had found this man and given him a piece of her mind!

But at the same time, as she neared the rock, she felt a wonderful feeling the likes of which she could not ever remember feeling before! It was a feeling of exhilaration mixed with self-respect and pride for what she had accomplished all by herself by coming here alone without any help from anyone else.

Finally, she could begin to make out what was written on the rock:

"Welcome young person of Wallaroo! I know why you have come here — because you were either too afraid or too lazy to pursue your dreams, and you went asking others for advice on how to live your life, and they told you to go see the Man on the Hill.

"The people of Wallaroo were originally very hard-working — they had to be in order to carve a clearing out of the wilderness and build a town where none had been before.

"But after the original inhabitants had finished their work and had begun to pass on their hard-acquired wealth to their children, they discovered that, far from making their children appreciate their parents more, receiving the fruits of their labors only made the children lazy, resentful, ungrateful, and unappreciative of what their parents had gone through to create such an easy life for their children.

"So the village elders got together and decided to come up with a way to help the young people of the village experience the special feeling of accomplishing something very difficult by themselves, hoping that once they had felt this special feeling they would be better able to decide how to live their lives.

"They knew that only people who were truly ready to take the necessary steps to becoming independent would make the decision to try to find the Man on the Hill and have the strength and courage to do so by themselves.

"Now, by coming here, you have proven, both to yourself and to every other adult in the village, that you can achieve what you set out to do.

"And when you return to the village, you will have gained not only the respect of the other people who came to see the Man on the Hill, but, more importantly, you will have gained your own self-respect and the confidence that you can become what you want to become.

"For if you had known before you left Wallaroo how hard the journey would be, you never would have attempted it.

"But now you know that even very difficult journeys can be completed, step by step by step.

"Never forget that no matter how hard it was for you to come here by yourself, it was a thousand times harder for your ancestors to leave their families and friends behind and come to this land and build your society.

"Most importantly, never ever tell anyone my secret, for all people must discover my secret by themselves."

It was signed, "The Man on the Hill," and, below that, the initials of hundreds of other people had been carved into the rock.

Stunned by what she had just learned, Jenny didn't know whether to dance with joy or cry with grief.

At first, she was angry that two of the people she had most trusted had lied to her in the way they did.

But as she sat at the base of the rock, reading the message over and over again, she began to understand and appreciate what great gifts not only her mother and Mr. Bramblebush but all of her forebears in the village had given her — not only the gifts of comfort and security but also the gifts of love for her and trust in her to choose and succeed at her own path in life.

When she knew that she had fully understood the message that the Man on the Hill had left for her, Jenny carved her own initials into the rock and began to skip happily down to the village.

Arriving home before her mother (for surely you don't think that, even in a fable, a mother would let her fifteen-year-old daughter spend a night alone in the hills, do you?), Jenny collapsed on her bed and fell fast asleep.

After she awoke, Jenny talked and talked to her mother, not only about her trip to see the Man on the Hill, but about all sorts of other important things, like her feelings about boys and her plans for the future. And her mother seemed to understand what Jenny was saying better than her mother had ever understood her before!

And after Jenny told all of the adults in Wallaroo that she had gone to see the Man on Hill, not only did they seem to treat her with more respect, but she began to treat them with more respect as well, for they all now shared the same secret of what one had to do to become (and be treated as) an adult.

She also felt much more energetic and better able to focus on her goals than she had been before she had spent the night on the hill.

And she knew that it would be a long hard path to get an engineering degree, and that the climb was probably closer to the size of a mountain than a hill.

But she also knew that if she started on her way, a path would appear to lead her and signs would appear to tell her if she was on the right course. And that, although it was a long path, if she just trusted herself, tried hard, and took it one step at a time, she would eventually reach her destination.

Jenny did get her degree in engineering, married, and had kids of her own.

And when, one by one, they reached that age when they told her they were bored and didn't know what to do with their lives, Jenny told them, just as her mother had told her, that they ought to go talk to the Man on the Hill.

It's easy to "plant a seed" but it takes a lot of care and patience to help it grow strong and tall...

The Child Grower

Mary, Mary, Quite Contrary was quite dissatisfied with her life.

For one thing, she was tired of having such a long name. When she filled out a form, she was never sure whether to list her last name as "Mary, Quite Contrary," "Quite Contrary," or just "Contrary." (Her friends all called her "Q.C.")

So the first thing she did was to legally change her last name to "Sunshine."

Then she started to re-evaluate other aspects of her life.

Mary had always enjoyed gardening (even though she was tired of people constantly asking her, "How does your garden grow?").

Now, she felt she had reached a point in her life when she wanted to raise something other than "silver bells and cockle shells" — she wanted to raise children. However, she had spent so much time tending to her garden that she hadn't a clue about how to do it, and she didn't want to raise garden-variety-type children; she wanted to raise the high-class gourmet kind that everyone would like.

So Mary did what any sensible girl would do: she looked in the yellow pages for an expert on "Child Growing." And right away she found what she was looking for, an ad for "Mother Nature's School of Organic Child Raising."

Mary made an appointment and rushed right over. (She hoped she wouldn't forget her new last name if they asked her to fill out any forms!)

But when she arrived, she was surprised to find nothing more than an old woman seated contentedly in a rocking chair in the shade of an elm tree. Hanging on a hook on the tree was a cellular phone.

The old woman was contentedly rocking back and forth, knitting a sweater.

"Are you 'Mother Nature'?" Mary asked contrarily.

"Yes, dear, I am," the old woman answered, putting down her knitting. "I've been looking forward to meeting you, Mary. Your gardening ability is well known hereabouts. How does your garden grow?"

Mary ignored the question and got right to the point.

"Mother Nature, I'm bored with raising vegetables and plants and things. I'm ready to raise children. Can you teach me how to do it?"

Well, Mother Nature rocked back and forth and smiled. She knew that not many girls thought so seriously about the matter beforehand, despite the fact that it was the most important job any man or woman would ever have in their lives.

"The recipe is not complicated," she began.

Hearing this, Mary drew closer and sat down on the grass beside Mother Nature.

"In fact, I've written the recipe on this piece of paper."

Mother Nature then reached in her pocket, took out a crumpled piece of paper, and handed it to Mary, who read it on the spot.

Mother Nature's Recipe

for Growing Good People

First, wait to have children until you are mature enough and emotionally and financially able to devote yourself to them. In other words, finish growing up, become independent, and bloom

yourself before trying to raise another person.

Second, find (or create) a healthy environment in which to grow them.

Third, make sure you choose a partner who cannot only provide good seed but will also be a good "co-gardener" to help you grow them.

Fourth, provide them with soil rich in culture, family and religion so they will grow roots that are long and strong.

Fifth, nourish them with a gentle rain of love mixed with a stiff dose of discipline so that they learn to appreciate both without taking the former for granted or feeling resentment toward the latter.

Sixth, fertilize them with a rich mixture of ideas and meaningful experiences. Help them develop a sense of respect, gratitude, self-discipline, duty, responsibility, awe, creativity, moral judgment, and generosity, and a love of learning.

Seventh, direct their growth in the "right" direction — toward the light of goodness — but also allow them to grow in new directions so long as they don't hurt themselves or others.

Eighth, protect them from the winds of bad societal influences as well as the "bites" of "predators." Give them the support that allows them to grow stronger and earn their own self-respect, but not so much that they become forever dependent on it.

Ninth, "prune" their bad habits early before the bad habits grow so heavy that they "break the back" of the growing person.

Last, take pride in how you have raised them but let them show off their own achievements; let them bloom, bask in the sunshine of other people's approval, and enjoy the fruits of their own labors.

Mary thanked Mother Nature, took the paper and hurried home.

Mary then proceeded to follow the directions on the paper carefully.

She waited until she was ready to marry, and then picked a good person to be her "co-gardener."

And the two of them succeeded in growing three respectful, loving, hard-working children.

But Mary (who was still a bit contrary) decided to keep her maiden name of "Sunshine."

Some things in life, like drugs, seem to offer us an easy way to forget our troubles. But, as the little girl in the following story discovers, forgetting our troubles doesn't make them go away...

The Sleep Mask

Jamilla had a hard life. She lived in the poorer section of the city, where there was a lot of crime and unemployment. Plus, ever since her parents had divorced, her father hardly ever came around, and her mother would just disappear for days at a time.

Some of the students at her junior high school managed by joining gangs. Others just seemed to ignore what was going on around them.

But Jamilla was not like the people in either of these groups. She didn't want to hurt anyone the way the gang members did, but at the same time she couldn't ignore things like the stronger kids did.

Jamilla felt so alone. In fact, she felt so bad that she had trouble sleeping at night, so she often fell asleep in class the next day, which only made her problems worse.

Then, one day, while staying home alone, she was so bored that she flipped through all of the UHF frequencies on her TV set to see if there were any new channels she hadn't seen before. (She liked to watch the foreign language programs, just to try to guess what they were talking about and to think about how people in other countries lived.)

Then, by chance, she saw a commercial on channel 77 that she had never seen before. It was an ad for the "Magimask," a sleep mask that was "guaranteed not only to help you sleep better but to make your pain disappear, too!" The mask was being demonstrated by a jolly-looking man wearing oversized pants and a colorful shirt. Best of all, the ad said the mask only cost a dollar and that there was a store not far from her house.

So Jamilla grabbed a dollar out of her mother's special hiding place, quickly hopped on her bike and tore over to the address she had written down.

And, sure enough, there was a store there with a big sign that read, "Sleep Aids!

Featuring the Revolutionary New MAGIMASK!"

Jamilla hopped off her bike and went inside.

There she found the same jolly-looking man wearing oversized pants and a colorful shirt that she had seen in the TV commercial.

"WhatcanIdoforya?" the man asked.

"I saw the ad for the Magimask on TV," explained Jamilla. "And I'd like to buy one," she said, holding out the dollar.

"Oh, you must have misunderstood," said the man. "We don't sell the Magimask, we rent it for the first night for one dollar."

"Oh," said Jamilla. Then, after thinking it over for a moment, she said, "OK, I'll rent it for one night, then."

"Goodgoodgood," say the jolly man. "But before I rent it to you, I have to explain how to use it.

"What you have to do is this: Before you put it on tonight, think about how you would like tomorrow to go for you, all of the things you hope will happen to you tomorrow. Then just put it on!"

"Great," said Jamilla, handing the dollar to the man.

But, as the man handed the mask to Jamilla, he warned, "Remember, a dollar only pays for one night, so you'll have to come back and pay me again if you want to use it again!"

"No problem," said Jamilla as she sped out the door, clutching the mask in her hand.

That night, before she went to sleep, Jamilla did just as the jolly man told her to do: she thought about how she would like the next day to go for her and all of the things she hoped would happen.

Then she put on the mask.

That night she slept better than she had slept in months, and when she woke up she felt better than she had in years.

And that day passed just as she had hoped that it would! She knew all of the answers on the test, talked back to and scared away the tough kids who always chased her on the playground, and that cute guy even said hello to her in the hall!

And when she got home, she discovered that the house was all painted and cleaned up, and that there was all new furniture, too.

Not only that, but her Mom and Dad were waiting for him. They told her that they had decided to get back together again and that her Dad had even gotten a good job!

Then they all sat down to the best meal and happiest evening she had ever known.

She was so happy that she had seen that commercial on TV!

But when she woke up the next morning, she found the house was back to just how it used to be, and her mother and father were nowhere to be seen!

"I must have been asleep for about 32 hours," thought Jamilla, "and I must have just been dreaming that everything had happened!"

So Jamilla grabbed the Magimask and hopped on her bike to took it back to the store.

But when Jamilla told the jolly man about what had happened, the man didn't seem surprised at all.

"Of course, that's the way Magimask is supposed to work!" he explained. "Didn't everything happen that you hoped would happen?"

"Yeah," admitted Jamilla, "but I was asleep for the whole time!"

"Well, would you like to rent it again?" asked the man.

Jamilla thought about it for a moment. She had already missed a whole day of school, so she wasn't exactly looking forward to going back and trying to explain that she had been asleep for 32 hours.

"I guess so, but I don't have a dollar with me. I'll have to go steal, I mean, get it."

"Oh, the second time you rent it, it costs two dollars, but it lasts for two whole days," the man explained.

"And the third time?" asked Jamilla.

"Three dollars and three days, and so on. Every time you rent it, it costs one more dollar but it works for one more day," was the answer.

"OK," said Jamilla, "I'll go get some money from my home."

But when Jamilla got home, she started to think about what she was doing. Was it a good idea to sleep through her life, even if her dreams were so much more pleasant than reality? And what if she liked the dreams so much that she kept using the Magimask — she'd need more and more money and spend more and more of her time asleep!

After thinking about this for a while, Jamilla decided that she would rather live her life, however painful it was, than to sleep through it.

So she went back to the store to tell the jolly man that she had changed her mind.

But when she got there, there was no sign of the store at all. In fact, there wasn't even a building!

Jamilla didn't know what to think about all of this, so she decided to leave.

When she got back home, she immediately turned on the television. And there on channel 77 was the same jolly man from the sleep aid store! He seemed to be looking right at Jamilla as he said:

"With the pleasure comes the pain,

With the effort comes the gain.

I will get what's coming to me

If I take responsibility."

When Jamilla heard this, she smiled, for she finally understood the secret of the "magimask."

And when the jolly man on TV saw Jamilla smile, he knew that Jamilla had understood his message, so he winked at Jamilla and disappeared, and Channel 77 turned to static.

Of course, Jamilla's life didn't change overnight, but she decided that if she studied real hard and worked real hard and took responsibility for her life that some day she might be able to create a real house and family like the one she had dreamed about.

And she did, and she did, and she did.

And she did!

Perhaps the best way to find a good person to share your life with is to act like the kind of person that a good person would be attracted to...

The Wise Old King

Once upon a time in the far away land of Laurania, there lived a wise, wealthy, and powerful ruler.

This King had but one son, the Crown Prince. He was a good lad, and brave and extremely handsome, but he had not yet shown (at least to his father's satisfaction) the kind of wisdom that a king should have.

One day the King decided that it was finally time for his son to end his playboy life and take a wife. So the King consulted with his ministers and, through their network of spies, learned that there was one maiden in the Kingdom who was known for her common sense and intelligence. In fact, all of the other maidens came to her for advice. Her name was Celia, and, although she was not exactly ugly, she was rather plain-looking. (She was also known to be quite stubborn and strong-willed.)

Now the King realized that the Crown Prince was also a very strong-willed young man and also had an eye for attractive young ladies, and he would never consent to marry anyone that his father had picked out for him.

So, the king came up with a plan.....

He instructed his ministers to bring to the court, one per night, all of the prettiest maidens in his Kingdom.

Before the first maiden was brought before him, however, the King had a talk with the Crown Prince.

"The choosing of a queen is a very serious matter," he admonished his son, "for not only your happiness but the future happiness of the entire Kingdom depends on the wisdom of your choice. And not only will you have to live with the woman you choose, but the children she bears for you will become the future rulers of our Kingdom. Choose wisely for it is perhaps the most important choice you will ever have to make."

The Crown Prince swore to his father that he would choose carefully and wisely.

So the nightly introductions began.

As each maiden was brought before the throne, the King told her sternly:

"As your King, I order you to spend the night with my son, the Crown Prince. If you refuse, I will forbid you from ever marrying anyone else, and you will live the rest of your days and nights as a single maid. But if you agree to do so and please him in the way he wishes to be pleased, you will become his bride and will be wealthy and contented for the rest of your life."

Well, this was not welcome news, and each maiden reacted with considerable consternation. (The Crown Prince, on the other hand, didn't seem too unhappy about it at all.) But faced with the choice of sleeping with the handsome Prince or lifelong spinsterhood, each lass agreed to spend the night with him, hoping to please him in the way he wished to be pleased and thus to live happily ever after.

And each night, from the Prince's bedroom could be heard the sounds of, shall we say, "glee."

But morning after morning, the young man sent each girl away, telling the King's nervous ministers that she had not pleased him in the way he wished to be pleased. And as time went on, the Prince seemed increasingly discouraged that he would ever find an appropriate mate.

Then one evening, the ministers brought before the throne another maiden. And although she was rather plain-looking, she had the pure innocent look of a child and she stood with the self-composed pride of a woman born with good character.

The Prince sat slumped in his chair, hardly seeming to be interested in the proceedings at all.

Then, for the umpteenth time, the King stated why he had had the maiden brought before him:

"As your King, I order you to spend the night with my son, the Crown Prince. If you refuse, I will forbid you from ever marrying anyone else, and you will live the rest of your days and nights as a single maid. But if you agree to do so and please him in the way he wishes to be pleased, you will become his bride and will be wealthy and contented for the rest of your life."

Hearing this, the young maiden's heart seemed to sink to the floor.

But quickly regaining her composure, she looked directly at the King and said:

"Sire, your wisdom is known far and wide, and I have always loved and respected you for it. But I would never sleep with a man under those conditions. For if I slept with him out of fear of never finding anyone else, it would be no different than if I let him rape me. And if I slept with him because of mere promises, I would be no better than a common whore.

"I would only sleep with a man if I deeply loved and cared for him in a long-term committed relationship and I knew that he felt the same way about me.

"I would rather never marry than lose my self-respect!"

Hearing these presumptuous words from a common girl, the King's ministers gasped and began to tremble, apparently fearing not only for the girl's safety but for their own as well!

The King, seemingly overcome with rage, sat speechless with his mouth agape. No one had ever spoken to him in such a way in his life!

But before the King could take any action, the Crown Prince stepped forward, took the maiden's hand, and spoke in a kind but firm voice:

"Father, I understand your good intentions. And I would be less than honest if I claimed not to have enjoyed these nightly auditions.

"But though I have gained a lot of, how shall I say it?... 'experience' these past few months, to tell you the truth, I have grown weary of feeling pleasure without feeling love at the same time.

"Now, after hearing these words from this fair maiden, I know that I have finally found the woman I have been looking for, one that I can share a life (and not just sex) with. For in speaking up in the honest way she did to you, she has shown that she is not only strong, wise, and brave, but that she will also be faithful to her husband just as she is faithful to her best self, no matter what riches she is offered or what loss she is threatened with.

"I will marry her not because of her outward appearance or because I expect her to cater to my every whim, but because I know I can trust and respect her!"

Thus the Crown Prince had not only found someone who would please him in the way he wished to be pleased. He had also shown that he was even wiser than his father and was not just some buffed-up hunk with his brains in his codpiece.

So all the Kingdom rejoiced, and the two married the following Spring.

But the one smiling most broadly at the wedding was the King, for only the King and his ministers knew that, as a result of the plan they had come up with, the Crown Prince had not only learned wisdom; he had also chosen as his bride the wisest maiden in the Kingdom, Celia.

Many girls wish for beauty, but they should be careful because they might just get what they wish for...

The Curséd Child

In the time before the Men of Iron ruled the earth there lived a maiden by the name of Letrice. She was the gentlest and comeliest maiden in all of Caladonia. She was also well looked after by the Goddess Aphrodite, who was, in fact, her own great-grandmother.

One day, while gathering flowers by the river Caladon, Letrice saw something the likes of which she had never seen before:

Two plants rose rapidly out of the ground, pushing the earth aside as if impatient to leave the earth and grow. Out of one of the plants a beautiful flower appeared, more beautiful than any Letrice had ever seen in her 17 years of life. Then out of the other plant, a plain-looking flower appeared. And as Letrice watched with moth agape, the beautiful flower wilted and fell to the ground, whereas the plain-looking flower quickly turned to seeds, and where the seeds fell to the ground, a dozen new plants sprang up before her widened eyes.

Scared by what was obviously a sign from the Gods, Letrice hurried to the Temple of Aphrodite where the seer Melancholia had in the past showed her great kindness. (She was called "Melancholia" because, when she was young, she was punished by the Gods for some oversight by being given the curses of both hindsight and foresight, and so she was forever full of regret and foreboding.)

After Letrice described what she had seen, Melancholia explained what it meant in her typically cryptic way:

"From two seeds in your field

Two flowers will grow.

One will be blesséd,

The other sorrow will know."

Letrice returned to her abode to ponder the significance of what Melancholia had told her.

Now, the great Zeus atop Mount Olympus was of course a God, but even Gods have their yearnings, and his all-seeing glance had not failed to notice the comely lass Letrice. And so it came to pass that one night, as his own wife Hera was away bringing succor to poor Atlas (who was doomed to hold the heavy weight of the sky upon his shoulders for all eternity), the great Zeus decided to pay a visit to the lovely Letrice as she prepared for bed.

When the magnificent God suddenly appeared before her, the innocent girl pulled back in fright.

"Do not fear, fair maiden," he comforted her, "for I have not come to harm you. Indeed, if you consent, I shall bring you pleasures the likes of which you have never before felt."

Now, even a well-brought-up girl finds it hard to resist the honey-coated words of a magnificent God, so before long the two of them were holding each other in an embrace so tight that even Hercules, the strongest of all mortals, could not have separated them.

In the morning, after having plowed her luscious furrow many times over, Zeus returned to his home atop Mount

Olympus, but not before planting a seed in the fertile field he left behind.

Unfortunately for Zeus, however, Hera had returned early from her journey, and had watched all that had transpired between Zeus and his mortal lover throughout the long hot night.

"I've warned you over and over about your unfaithful ways!" Hera screamed at her roving husband upon his return from his earthly dalliance.

But Zeus smugly replied: "You know you cannot punish me except with barbed words, for not only am I one of the Twelve Immortals, but I am in fact the strongest God of all."

"Then I shall punish the one who has insulted me!" Hera threatened.

And then, faster than a hawk swoops down to take its prey in its talons did Hera fly down to the bedroom of the unsuspecting Letrice.

The girl was just awakening with a smile on her face, wondering if the pleasure she had experienced during the night was merely a foolish dream placed into her mind by the impish god Pan. However, when Letrice saw Hera standing there, she knew that it had been no dream at all, and, fearing Hera's retribution, she pulled her bed coverings up in front of her naked body as if to shield herself from the wrath of the Queen of the Gods.

"Fear not, fair one," began Hera soothingly, "for I do not entirely blame you for my husband's transgressions. I have been married to him long enough to know not to trust in his fidelity and to know that few maidens are able to resist his wiles. However," she said, her voice becoming more ominous, "I cannot allow the seed that is within you to go untouched. And so

I shall curse the child that is born from it to live a life of pain and sorrow."

And with that, Hera returned to Mount Olympus, leaving the bewildered and grieving girl alone to ponder the fate of her unborn child.

However, just as Hera was well aware of her husband's roving ways, so too was Zeus aware of his wife's jealousy, and he had watched and listened to her meeting with Letrice from his throne high atop the Home of the Gods. And as soon as Hera had left his paramour of the night before, the Son of Cronos once again came to comfort her as best he could.

When Letrice saw him, she fell crying into his majestic arms. But he pushed her back so he could look deep into her tear-stained eyes, and then he spoke to her in soothing tones:

"I know what curse my wife has lain upon the seed growing within you, and I cannot undo what she has done," he explained, thinking of the mischief that Hera and her minions could cause him. "However, this I can do: beside that curséd seed I will place another, a sister who will be equally blesséd as her sister is curséd." And this he proceeded to do.

Then, after giving Letrice one final hug, the Great God wiped the tears from her face and used them to water the side of Mount Olympus. And, where before there had been nothing but rocks and harpies' nests, a beautiful willow tree sprang up from each place where one of her tears fell on the slope.

And so it came to pass that after nine new moons had crawled across the sky, Letrice gave birth to the two girls, one blesséd and one curséd.

And indeed, as sure as Cerberus the three-headed dog guards the gates to the Under-world, one child, Pamela, grew up fair and lovely and the other, Hillary, grew up plain.

Many long years did Letrice labor in solitude to raise the two girls, for she could find no man who would risk the wrath of the Gods that would fall upon him if he made a mistake in raising their children.

And many a night, recalling the seer's solemn prophecy, did Letrice wail and pull at her hair in grief that, due to her lack of judgment and wanton act, she alone was responsible for bringing into the world and raising a child as curséd as poor Hillary.

And, as happens when a pretty girl flowers into her womanhood, Pamela had many suitors who wished to introduce her to the gifts of Eros. But poor Hillary was left alone. And you can be sure that Pamela rarely failed to remind the stolid Hillary of that fact.

And, as happens when one is as lovely as Pamela, she soon was with child, and then another and another. But as, in time, she slowly lost her beauty, fewer and fewer men came calling until, by the time she was approaching her thirtieth birthday, she was a poor, uneducated, tired and husbandless hag, forever chasing her numberless children and cleaning up after them.

And as her children grew, they turned out to be so ill-bred that, one by one, they died untimely deaths, leaving Pamela to grow old all alone in the world.

Meanwhile, Hillary, because of her uncommonly plain looks, had been forced to develop her knowledge, personality and talents so that by the time she was thirty she was much admired not only by mortal men but by the Gods as well. In fact, so taken was Zeus with Hillary that he arranged for her to meet and marry Larriscus, the one man in his earthly domain who was equal in talent and goodness to this plain-looking lass. And the two of them succeeded in raising four hard-working children who bestowed upon them the greatest gift of all, loving grand-children.

Letrice, now approaching her seventieth birthday, was much puzzled by this turn of events, so she once again went to the Temple of Aphrodite to inquire of the now-agéd Melancholia.

"I do not understand the ways of the Gods," began Letrice, "for my daughter Pamela, born blesséd of them, has of late seen nothing but woe, and my daughter Hillary, the curséd one, has of late had her life filled with joy and contentment. Does this mean that the Gods, in all their wisdom, repented and withdrew their original curses and decided to give to whom was born with nothing and to take from whom was born with plenty?"

"No, not all," explained Melancholia. "You still have not understood my original prophecy at all. For you see, when Hera cursed your child, it was in fact Pamela who was the unfortunate one, for Hera cursed her with great but temporary beauty so that she would never develop the talents needed to live a rich and fulfilling life. And when Zeus, in his matchless wisdom, put within you the seed of another child, it was indeed Hillary's seed that he placed there. And he blessed her with such plainness that she would be forced to develop her talents and wisdom, aspects of her character which have served her well and which will bring her happiness for the rest of her days."

And it was only then that Pamela understood that, as indeed it had been in her own life, beauty can be the greatest curse of all, for although it can bring early attention, it can also bring long-lasting grief and loneliness.

Life can be a long lonely scary voyage over uncharted waters but we do not sail alone.

Those we left behind us still cheer for our success as those do who await our arrival...

The Torch Bearer

Michelle Seaver wobbled as she stood, bleary-eyed, looking down from the top of the clock tower of her high school.

Although her school was originally built in the 1930s, it had been renovated and expanded many times. For example, concrete bleachers had been built by the football field in the 1970s and an Olympic-size swimming pool had been added in the 1980s.

The clock tower, however, had remained unchanged ever since it had been completed in 1933.

Some people in the community worried that someday someone might try to commit suicide by jumping from the top of the tower, and they wanted to have it closed off, but the School Board saw no reason to spend the money to do so because it had never happened.

Yet.

Michelle took another drink from the bottle of whiskey that she had smuggled out of her parents' liquor cabinet. Although she had only lived for sixteen years, she had had enough of life. She was tired of the pain and the isolation and the not knowing who she was and where she was going.

She was also tired of her parents being mad at her all the time. She was doing the best she could. What more did they want from her?

She had tried to make friends, but one group seemed too snobbish and another seemed too wild. The nerds were too boring and she couldn't stand being around the groupies who hung around when the athletes practiced.

No way was she gonna hang out with the druggies, and she sure didn't want to hang out with the blacks, Latinos, or Asians — no minority friends for her.

Finally she had just started to dress in black and hang around with the Goths. That had only made her more depressed, but at least she didn't feel so lonely when she was with them.

She had thought about suicide many times and had wondered which way would be the least painful way to do it, but today, after getting another "D" in math, and then getting the news that she had dreaded — that she was, indeed, pregnant — she had finally decided to "take the plunge." She figured that if she was drunk enough, she would hardly feel the pain as she hit the ground.

The openings in tower next to the clock were very narrow, however, and she began to worry that she might not be able to squeeze through one of them. (That was another thing she hated about herself: she was too fat.) But she decided to try anyway.

She put down the bottle and had just started to try to squeeze through one of the openings when she was startled to hear a man's voice.

"Hey, what're you doing there!"

When she turned her head, she saw an old man standing behind her. He had a long white beard and was dressed in a dusty robe, like a monk.

"Who are you?" she asked, startled.

"I'm the keeper of the tower. Now come out of there," he said as he pulled her back from the opening.

"The keeper of the tower?" she said. "I thought that was just a story that the upper classmen told the freshmen."

"Story or no, here I am," he said. "Now what are you doing here?"

Michelle looked down. "I was just...." Her voice trailed off.

"Look, it's no business of mine what you want to do with your life," the old man said, "but whatever you were going to do today you can do tomorrow. So, before you do something you won't live to regret, all I ask is that you take a little walk with me."

By this point Michelle couldn't argue, so she just silently nodded and followed the old man as he led her down the steps.

It was already quite late, so when they got to the bottom of the tower, the campus was empty. An eerie fog was coming in that obscured the late afternoon sun.

"Where're we going?" Michelle asked.

"Just follow me," the old man said.

So she followed him as he led her to the football field.

And when they got there, she was surprised to see hundreds of people in the stands.

Then her surprise turned to shock when, in the front row of the bleachers on one side of the football field, she saw her parents! Why were they here?

But she almost fainted when, in the row behind her parents, she saw her four grandparents, including her mother's father, who had died before Michelle was born!

In the next row sat eight people, and sixteen in the next row up, and so on, until the top row was fully occupied with people from left to right.

But the strangest thing was that, as she looked up in succeeding rows, the people's clothes got more and more old-fashioned, until in the last row at the top many of the people were dressed like eighteenth century peasants or farmers. As she her eye followed the rows up to the top, she also saw a whole group of black people sitting there.

Michelle turned to ask the old man what was going on, but before she could voice the words, he put his finger to his lip and "hushed" her.

"Now listen, Michelle." (How did he know her name?, she wondered.) "The people on this side are all your ancestors — not only your parents and their parents, but their parents, and so on.

"See up in row six?" (The people in the sixth row all stood up.) "That's James T. Wilmington on the right." (James doffed his hat shyly.) "He suffered terribly sailing around the Horn to get to California before all the gold ran out.

"And next to him is Mittie Fairwell." (Mittie, a black woman, smiled self-consciously.) "Why, you can't imagine the hardships she suffered in her life, first as a slave and then as a runaway, making her way, all by herself, all the way across the country from South Carolina to end up working as a laundrywoman in California before she met your great-great-great-great-great grandfather James."

James and Mittie looked lovingly at each other and then started to hold hands.

"Can you imagine how much they suffered — a white man and a black woman in nineteenth century America?

"Betty and Willie Tarrington, meanwhile, were making their way across the country in a wagon train. They got stuck in the middle of the dessert and Willie died, but Betty was already pregnant with your great-great-great-great grandmother, and she somehow managed to have the baby and survive on her own in Nevada.

"Walter Gustaf, on the other hand, fled religious persecution in Germany by stowing away on a merchant ship. When he was found out, the captain had him whipped mercilessly, but he survived to jump ship in Boston."

Walter grimaced, remembering the pain of the voyage to America.

"And Jeddadiah Smith died fighting in the Civil War, leaving a pregnant wife and three small children behind. Can you imagine how much she struggled to keep those four kids alive?"

And so the old man continued, going up row by row, describing to Michelle all the hardships her ancestors had suffered just to survive so that, eventually, she could be standing there....

When the old man had finished describing the people in the stands, he turned to Michelle and said:

"You see, Michelle, you come from a line of winners, people who didn't give up, no matter what pain, fear or hardship they suffered. Every single one of your ancestors somehow managed to live long enough to pass his or her life on to a child who would be another one of your ancestors."

Michelle, shocked and moved, looked down, trying to hold back the tears.

"I... I never knew that so many people had gone to so much effort and had suffered so much just so..."

"The flame of your life," the old man continued, "was lit long before you were born, and was carried with great effort down through the ages so that it could be given to you to carry and pass on."

And then her tears began to flow.

After a few minutes, she raised her head and looked over at the other side of the field. The fog had come in so she couldn't see the people clearly, but she could see that, the same as in the bleachers behind her, there were a few people in the bottom row, a few more behind them in the next row, and so on, until the top row was full of people.

"And who are they?" she asked the keeper of the tower.

"Why, those are your descendants," he answered. "That is, if you decide to stick around a while."

She stared at them in shocked disbelief.

"You see, you are only link between all the people on that side" (He gestured to all of her ancestors behind her in the first set of bleachers.) "and all the people on that side."
(He gestured to all of her descendants in the other bleachers.) "It's up to you to carry the torch across."

"Now you can do what you want with your life — that's up to you — but if you do what you were planning to do, that spark of life growing inside of you will never get to shine. All of the people on that side will never have the opportunity to experience the life — with all its triumphs and hardships and pain — that was given

106

to you and which you were planning to throw away. They'll just fade into the fog and disappear."

The combination of the booze and the shock of what she was experiencing was now getting to Michelle, and she slumped to the ground.

"Now, I have to get back to my duties, making sure no one else is up to any mischief in the tower," the old man said, "but you just stay here if you want until you feel strong enough to go.

"And, by the way... If you decide you still want to try squeeze through that narrow opening, well, the next time I won't try to stop you."

With that, the man turned and walked away and soon disappeared into the fog.

Michelle stood there in a daze, not sure what to do.

Then her parents stood up and her father said, "You can do it, Michelle!"

And then her grandparents stood and cheered, and then her great-grandparents, and row-by-row the entire stand-full of people stood up in a wave of support that stretched back to eternity, cheering for her success.

Then, from behind her, came the sound of all of her descendents, standing and cheering as well.

Michelle got dizzy looking back and forth between all the people on both sides of
the field cheering for her.

Exhausted, she closed her eyes, lay down and soon fell asleep....

When she woke up, it was already dark, so she got up and hurried home.

She knew her parents would be worried and mad at her for being late (not to mention the fact that she was pregnant!) but, somehow, now she didn't mind.

In the "Child Grower," a young girl learned that one must be patient to raise a child.

In the following two stories, two girls learn that "you can't hurry love," and shouldn't try to.

The Make-Up Artist

Maria was not exactly bad-looking, but she wasn't the kind of girl who turned heads when she walked down the hall at her high school either. She was popular and active and had a lot of girl friends and all that, but she couldn't seem to get any boy interested in her romantically.

Of course, there was her next-door neighbor, Fred, but she had known him since they were both in pre-school together, and he was just, well, "just Fred." They would sometimes go to a movie or ice skating, but just as "friends." You know what I mean.

And when she had a problem that she couldn't discuss with anyone else, not her parents, not her sisters, not even her girl friends, she always felt comfortable discussing it with Fred.

She was friendly with other boys in school, too, but they were all the boring nerdy types who would rather spend a Saturday night studying or practicing their music than going out dancing.

The one guy she really liked, Rick, didn't even seem to notice her. He was a really cool guy who wore cool clothes, drove a cool car, and hung out with other cool guys. But the only time Maria saw Rick was in the halls between classes because she was in the advanced classes and Rick was taking auto shop or driver's ed or something.

One day, talking to her girl friend Josephine, Maria asked, "Josephine, how come you get all the guys and I'm always home alone on Saturday night? You're not that much better looking than I am."

Josephine laughed and said, "You're right, I'm not. But I use make-up and I spend a lot of money on my hair and my clothes. You need to do something to fix up your appearance, girl!"

"You really think so?" asked Maria.

"I know so," responded Josephine.

So, with Josephine's guidance, Maria got a fancy haircut. She also got some make-up and sexy clothes, but she left those things at Josephine's house so her parents wouldn't find out. She would get up early, put on a scarf, and leave her house an hour earlier than usual so she could stop by Josephine's house to change into her new clothes and put on her make-up before going to school.

And, sure enough, from the first day, Maria started getting noticed by the boys. And before she knew it, Rick had asked her for a date!

So the next Saturday night she told her parents that she was going to go visit Josephine. But when she got there, she changed into her sexy clothes and put on her make-up, and Rick showed up at Josephine's house to pick her up.

But the date didn't go well at all.

First of all, she and Rick didn't have anything in common. (To tell you the truth, he was kind of a dufus.) All he wanted to talk about, or apparently could talk about, was cars: how to fix them, how to paint them, how to race them, and how to steal them.

And what was worse, he couldn't keep his hands off of Maria. He kept trying to get her to get into the back seat of the car with him.

Finally, she couldn't stand it any longer and told him, "Look, if you can't stop trying to crawl all over me, I'm going to get out and call my parents!"

"Whadya mean?" responded Rick. "Don't you put out?"

"No!" replied Maria.

"Well, all of the other girls who dress like you do put out."

"I'm not that kind of girl!" declared Maria.

"So why do you dress like that kind of girl?" asked Rick, truly puzzled.

Maria wasn't sure what the answer to that question was, but she asked Rick to take her back to Josephine's house, and he did.

When she got to Josephine's, she could hardly hide her tears. Without answering Josephine's questions, she quickly took off her make-up, changed her clothes, and headed back home.

While walking down her street, she ran into Fred, who was just coming back from the library.

"Hi, Maria," he called out in his friendly way, "Whacha doing?"

"Nothing," said Maria miserably.

"Well, I don't have any plans either. Do you want to go see a movie or something?"

Maria stopped and looked at him for a moment.

Then, finally, she said, "Sure, why not? What movie do you want to see? I heard the new Spielberg is really good."

"Yeah, that's sounds great," answered Fred. "Let me drop off these books first and I'll be right out."

"And I'll go tell my parents where I'm going," said Maria, happily.

And that night, for the first time, Maria didn't think of Fred as "just Fred."

And that night, for the first time, Fred told Maria that she looked "kinda pretty."

The Late Bloomer

Jane was smart and a very good person. But she was plain. That's why everyone called her "Plain Jane." (At least that's what they called her behind her back.)

Although Jane was 16 years old, she had never had a boyfriend, and, as you can imagine, she was quite upset about it!

She especially liked Billy Anderson, but he was always chasing the pretty girls, like that cheerleader, Karen Linder.

So just like Mary, Mary, Quite...er, I mean, just like Mary "Sunshine," Jane decided to look in the phone book for help.

And, sure enough, under the heading "People Growing," she found what she was looking for, an ad for "Mother Nature's Beauty School."

And just like Mary, Mary,...er, Mary What's-Her-Name, Jane made an appointment and rushed right over.

But when she arrived at the address that was listed for "Mother Nature's Beauty School," Jane was surprised to find nothing more than an old woman contentedly knitting in a rocking chair in the shade of an elm tree. Hanging on a hook on the tree was a cellular phone.

"Are you 'Mother Nature'?" Jane asked plainly.

"Yes, dear, I am," the old woman answered, putting down her knitting. "I've been looking forward to meeting you, Jane. I hear you have quite an interest in planes."

Mary ignored that comment and got right to the point.

"Mother Nature, I'm 16 years old and I still don't have a boy friend. Can you help me?"

Mother Nature rocked back and forth and smiled. She knew that many girls thought much too much about that matter, despite the fact that there was no hurry for them to do so.

So Mother Nature leaned forward, looked right in Jane's face, and said seriously, "Now I have the solution for your problem, but you have to do exactly as I say!"

Jane promised Mother Nature that she would.

So Mother Nature leaned over and pulled a small bag out of a bigger bag sitting on the ground next to her.

"Now listen carefully," she began. "In this bag are some wildflower seeds. I want you to spread these seeds in your front yard, and then do nothing, just watch what happens in the Spring and Summer. Then come back to see me in the Autumn and tell me what you observed. I'll be here."

And with that, she went back to her knitting.

Jane took the bag, even though she couldn't see how planting some stupid seeds was going to help her get a boyfriend.

But when she got home, she made some phone calls around town and found out that Mother Nature had a good reputation for success.

So Jane did as Mother Nature had advised her to do, and she planted the seeds. And Jane watched what happened in the Spring and Summer, and then went back to see Mother Nature in the Fall.

A big smile broke out on Mother Nature's face as soon as she saw Jane, and she immediately asked Jane to tell her what she had observed.

"Well, at first nothing happened. Then in April, some yellow flowers came out and bloomed. Then in May some little orange flowers came out and bloomed. In June, some big white ones came out and bloomed, and in August some more of the yellow ones came out," Jane said curtly. She didn't see what this was supposed to prove.

But then Mother Nature explained: "You see, Jane, there is a season for every living thing, and every living thing blossoms when their time comes, without us having to do anything about it at all. You just have to be patient and believe that your time to bloom will come."

But Jane was still not convinced, so Mother Nature leaned over and picked up a seedling that was on the ground next to her.

"Now, Jane," she began, "I want you to trust me and to promise me, cross your heart, that you will do exactly as I tell you to do."

Jane wanted to hear what the proposal was before making any promises.

"Now, what I want you to do is these three things," continued Mother Nature, handing the little tree to Jane.

"First of all, I want you to plant this tree and to take care of it so that it grows up healthy and straight.

"Then I want you to promise me not to worry about finding a boy friend until this tree blooms.

"Last, I want you to promise me that you will also not look in any mirrors until this tree blooms. Do you understand? Because if you look in a mirror, it will break the magic and the spell won't work."

Well, Jane sighed and looked down. But she decided she would give the old lady's advice one more try, so she crossed her heart and promised to do just as Mother Nature had asked her to do.

And as Jane left, Mother Nature called out to her, "I guarantee you it will work, Jane!"

Then she went back to her knitting.

So Jane went home, and planted the tree.

The next thing she did was put away all of the mirrors in her house.

And she tried, the best she could, not to worry about getting a boyfriend.

So Jane took care of the tree year after year, but year after year it didn't bloom.

Jane was an honorable person, however, so while she tended to the tree, she went to and graduated from college, got a master's degree, and then a good job, without looking in a mirror once!

A couple times she felt so desperate that she almost agreed to marry the "wrong" person, but, keeping her faith in the promises made by Mother Nature, she didn't do so.

But then one Saturday, after she had tended to the tree for almost ten years and had almost given up hope of ever getting married, Jane was working in the front yard when a man walked by.

He stopped in front of her, and asked her jokingly, "How does your garden grow?" (Although he was a nice guy, he didn't have a good pick-up line because he rarely tried to hit on girls anymore.)

Jane looked up and smiled at the silliness of the question.

Then they got to talking, and, what do you know! It was none other than Billy Anderson, the boy Jane had liked from afar in high school! He had married Karen Linder soon after graduation, but, well, you know how it is, they had grown in different directions and there had been some infidelity.

So they got divorced after only two years.

But Billy had matured considerably because of the experience.

For one thing, because of his experience in the marriage, he had learned that beauty is only skin deep, and that there are more important things (such as character, honesty, and maturity) to look for in a partner than a pretty face and someone who is good in bed.

He had also learned that to be happy in life, it is not a choice of sleeping with one woman or many women; it is a matter of finding and staying with the right woman.

He was also finally making enough money to support a family.

Well, one thing led to another, and after dating an appropriate length of time and getting to know each other real well, Billy asked Jane to marry him. Jane, however, ever loyal to her promise to Mother Nature, told him that she needed some time to think about it.

But, lo and behold, the next time she went to water the tree, you guessed it, it was blooming!

So the first thing Jane did was run to the closet and take out one of the mirrors that she had put away over ten years earlier. After ten years, you can imagine how eager she was to see what she looked like!

But when she looked in the mirror, she didn't recognize the face that she saw looking back at her at all!

For the last time she had looked in a mirror, about the time she had gone to visit Mother Nature, she had seen the face of an immature and plain teenage girl looking back at her.

But there in the mirror now was the face of a mature, attractive, and accomplished young woman!

So Mother Nature was right after all...

Jane had bloomed just in time, in the season that she was meant to bloom.

And then she got married, in the right season of her life to the right person.

Sometimes the most powerful effect of a drug is the so-called "placebo effect," that is, the effect that we think it's supposed to have...

The Spicist

There were five girls in Mrs. McGillicuddy's fourth grade class who were inseparable: Caitlin, Latasha, Gloria, Masako, and Katya.

Like all the other girls their age, they dreamed of "having it all" when they grew up: a handsome husband, a career and a family at the same time.

They hung out together in elementary school, they hung out together in junior high school, they hung out together in high school.

They even hung out together in junior college.

After junior college they went their separate ways, but they kept in touch, through marriages and divorces, new jobs and lay-offs.

Now they were pushing 30, however, and all they had to show for their years of relationships and hard work were condos that were worth less than they had paid for them, and balances on their credit card statements that could have sunk the Titanic.

Three of them had married and divorced, and the other two hadn't married at all.

So, at their monthly get-together, they were all unhappy for one reason or another.

Caitlin, for example, felt that, due to a lack of energy, she had fallen behind in her career.

Latasha had been assaulted, so she got panic attacks whenever she went out in public.

Masako felt that she just wasn't smart enough to compete.

For her part, Katya was always busy running around and never seemed to find the time to accomplish everything she wanted to accomplish.

And Gloria was just depressed.

Although the five of them enjoyed getting together once a month, afterwards they just went back to their lives and their problems, and nothing seemed to change.

Then one day, while walking down a street that she hadn't walked down in some time, Caitlin noticed a new shop. The only sign on the shop was a hand-painted one that read, "Mama Jamaica, the Spicist." Below that was written: "Try my drinks to cure your problems and spice up your life!"

Well, Caitlin had heard of "herbalists" before who sold herbs to cure problems, but she had never heard of a "spicist" before.

So, intrigued, she entered the store. In the store, she found nothing: just a chair, a counter, and empty shelves with not a thing on them.

But just as she turned to leave, she heard a cheery voice from over her shoulder calling to her in a lilting Caribbean accent.

"Welcome to my spice shop!" the voice said.

When Caitlin turned around, she saw standing behind the counter a big dark-skinned woman with an even bigger smile. "What can I do for you?" the woman asked. "Do you have any problems that you need solved?"

"No, not really," answered Caitlin. "I just stopped in because I was intrigued by your sign." And again Caitlin turned and started to leave.

"Not so fast, my dear," called out the woman. "If you don't have any problems, you must be the only person in the world who doesn't. Why don't you tell Mama Jamaica just one problem that you have?"

For a moment, Caitlin froze in the doorway, unsure whether to leave or to respond. But she was so unhappy with her life that she thought, "What have I got to lose?"

So she turned around, sat down in the chair, and began to tell Mama Jamaica about her feeling that she would never get ahead due to a lack of energy.

Hearing this, Mama Jamaica immediately said, "Just a minute," and disappeared into the back room.

After about a minute she came out with a paper cup that had the word "Ketchup" written on it.

"Drink this," she commanded. "It will help you to 'catch up' in your career."

Even though she thought the whole thing was silly, Caitlin drank what was in the cup. It tasted spicy but not too bad.

Still skeptical, she asked Mama Jamaica how much she owed her.

But Mama Jamaica said not to worry, that she had just opened and was trying to get new business, so she was giving away free samples.

So Caitlin thanked her and went home.

And, wouldn't you know it, she did start to feel better. She started to work out every day, and she found that she had more energy to get her work done. She even started to stay after work to get ahead in her assignments.

And soon her boss noticed how much she was doing and recommended her for a promotion and a raise!

So the next time Caitlin met with her four friends, she told them about the spice shop and how much the "ketchup" drink had helped her. They, of course, were all skeptical, but they each agreed to go visit Mama Jamaica and see if she had anything that could help them.

First, Latasha went there. And after Mama Jamaica listened to her story about being assaulted and how afraid she was to go out any more, the woman once again said, "Just a minute," and disappeared into the back room.

After about a minute she came out with a paper cup that had the word "Mace" written on it.

"Drink this," she commanded. "It will help you to become less afraid."

Even though Latasha thought the whole thing was silly, she drank what was in the cup. It tasted spicy but not too bad.

Still skeptical, Latasha asked Mama Jamaica how much she owed her.

But Mama Jamaica said not to worry, that she had just opened and was trying to get new business, so she was giving away free samples.

So Latasha thanked her and went home.

And, wouldn't you know it, she did start to feel more self-confident! So she started to take courses in self-defense at the local

"Y", and for the first time in years felt less afraid to go out in public!

Next, it was Masako's turn.

She went to the shop and told Mama Jamaica about her feelings of inferiority about her intelligence. And Mama Jamaica once again disappeared into the back room and soon reappeared with a paper cup that had the word "Sage" written on it.

"Drink this," she commanded. "It will make you smarter."

Well, even though Masako thought the whole thing was silly, she drank what was in the cup. It tasted spicy but not too bad.

Still skeptical, Masako asked Mama Jamaica how much she owed her.

But Mama Jamaica said not to worry, that she had just opened and was trying to get new business, so she was giving away free samples.

So Masako thanked her and went home.

And, wouldn't you know it, she did start to feel more intelligent! So she started to read more and then she decided to take some courses at the local college in order to finally get her bachelor's degree.

And, for the first time in years, she wasn't so afraid to get into intellectual discussions with other people!

Next, it was Katya's turn.

She went to the shop and told Mama Jamaica about her feelings that she never had enough time to do everything that she wanted to do. And Mama Jamaica once again disappeared into the back room and soon reappeared with a paper cup that had the word "Thyme" written on it.

"Drink this," she commanded. "It will help you find more time in your life."

Even though Katya thought the whole thing was silly, she drank what was in the cup. It tasted spicy but not too bad.

Still skeptical, Katya asked Mama Jamaica how much she owed her.

But Mama Jamaica said not to worry, that she had just opened and was trying to get new business, so she was giving away free samples.

So Katya thanked her and went home.

And, wouldn't you know it, she did start to feel more settled! So she started to get her life organized. She started to make lists and to prioritize what she had to do.

And, for the first time in years, she managed to get everything done and still have some time left over to enjoy herself!

Last, it was Gloria's turn.

She went to the shop and told Mama Jamaica about her feelings of depression. And Mama Jamaica once again disappeared into the back room and soon reappeared with a paper cup that had the word "Relish" written on it.

"Drink this," she commanded. "It will help you to enjoy life more."

Even though Gloria thought the whole thing was silly, she drank what was in the cup. It tasted spicy but not too bad.

Still skeptical, Gloria asked Mama Jamaica how much she owed her.

But Mama Jamaica said not to worry, that she had just opened and was trying to get new business, so she was giving away free samples.

So Gloria thanked her and went home.

And she did start to feel more hopeful about her life! So she started to get out more, she joined some clubs, and she started to do some volunteer work at the local hospital.

And, for the first time in years, she started to enjoy her life!

Well, naturally, the next time the five women got together they compared stories, and they were all thrilled to hear how well the other women's lives were going.

So they made a plan to go as a group to visit Mama Jamaica and thank her.

But when they entered the spice shop and called out, "Mama Jamaica!", there was no response. Fearing that something might be wrong, they walked behind the counter and into the back room.

A Reggae song was playing in the background:

"You can do what you wanna doooooo....

"You can be what you wanna beeeeee.....

"All you gotta dooooo is belieeeeeeeve......"

All over the back room there were paper cups and marker pens.

And sitting on a table in the rear of the room was a large bottle, with "Mama Jamaica's All-Spice Cure-All Potion" written on the label.

Someone suggested that they try it, so, one by one, they did.

It tasted spicy but not too bad.

Studies have shown that a child's behavior is directly related to an adult's expectations.

So wouldn't it be better if we expected good things of every child?

The Secret of Her Success

It was only after Miss Craig had retired that her former students found out that she had been lying to them for all those years.

Miss Craig had worked as an elementary school teacher for over 35 years and was known all over the city for producing, year after year, the best students, students who went on to outshine their contemporaries all through their school years and into their professional lives. People often asked her to tell them the secret of her success as a teacher, but she would just smile and say that it was no secret — she just had wonderful students.

Miss Craig never did marry — she always said that since she felt so fulfilled teaching her students that there wasn't any room in her heart for anyone else. And her students loved her back. In fact, they would come back to see her from time to time, even after they too had grown up and had kids of their own.

Over the years, Miss Craig had taught close to a thousand students, so when word spread in the city that Miss Craig was about to retire, many of her older former students got in touch with one another and planned a retirement party for her.

The party took place in the American Legion Hall, and more than a hundred of her former students showed up. A table, chairs, and a lectern were set up on the stage on the west side of the hall, and seven of her former students shared the stage with her.

After dinner, it was time for the speeches. The first to speak was Jeremy Conrad:

"Folks, no need to go into why we're here — we're here to salute the best teacher

this city ever had."

Applause filled the room as Miss Craig uncomfortably tried to accept all the praise they were offering her.

"However, I have a confession to make: I have decided to do something that I promised I never would do — I'm going to break a promise that I made to Miss Craig many years ago when I was in her class."

Miss Craig looked surprised and again shifted uncomfortably on her chair as she awaited Jeremy's revelation.

"You see, before I had been in Miss Craig's class, I had had some problems in school — nothing too serious, just schoolboy-foolin'-around type stuff. I just didn't take school very seriously, I guess. The truth is, no one in my family had ever gone to college, and education just wasn't emphasized in my family very much.

"Anyway, one day during the first few weeks of school, Miss Craig pulled me aside. She told me she wanted to talk to me privately because she had something important to tell me.

"She sat me down and, after she was sure that I was paying attention to what she was saying, she began.

"She told me that she had been observing me in class, and that she had noticed something about me. But, before she told me what it was, she made me swear never to tell any of the other kids because they would just get jealous and feel like I was the teacher's pet or something.

"So, after I crossed my heart and gave her my word that I would keep the secret and never reveal it to anyone, she told me what the secret was.

"She told me that because she had taught school for so many years she had developed a kind of psychic ability, a kind of sixth sense, that she could see people's futures, and that as soon as I had come into her class she had noticed that I was different from the other kids and that I was one of those kids destined to take a special path in life. She told me that she could tell by the way I acted and by the way I spoke and even by the way I walked that I had great undiscovered potential, potential that even I didn't realize I had, and that if I just applied myself and tried hard that I would be able to achieve great things in my life.

"I'll never forget what she told me that day. She looked me right in the face and said, 'Remember, Jeremy, I know. I know. I've taught hundreds of students, and I know. I have a special ability to see these things. Just by looking at you I know that you are different from all of the other kids — you have a special destiny and you have special abilities that you must cherish and develop so that you can use those special abilities to some day give something special back to the world.'"

"And, as some of you already know, I went on to become the first person in my family ever to graduate from college."

By this time, there wasn't a dry eye in the house, so Jeremy quietly walked over, gave Miss Craig a hug, and then retook his seat.

The next speaker, Jawon Johnson, then stepped up to the lectern and began to speak:

"You know, it's quite a coincidence, really, that you told that story, because when I was in Miss Craig's class several years after you were, she told me the same thing!"

There was a moment of silence in the hall, and then Mary Cullinski spoke up from the audience and said, "Yeah, and she told me that too!"

And then Sol Shapiro stood up and shouted, "She told me the same thing!"

And, before you knew it, one by one, all of Miss Craig's former students realized what she had done, and they laughed and shouted out one by one, "Me, too!"

And it was at that moment that they finally realized what the secret of her success was: she had made each of her students feel special and feel like they could become successful if only they believed in themselves.

And then, although all of her former students who were gathered there that day realized that Miss Craig had, in a way, lied to each and every one of them, they once again stood as a group and saluted her with a thunderous ovation for having been such a wonderful teacher. And, as Miss Craig sat on the stage beaming with pride, she tried unsuccessfully to hide a blush — the simplicity of her "secret" had finally been revealed.

The following story is not about how a woman should lead her life. Rather, it is about the crippling effects of smoldering anger and how it sometimes keeps us from doing the things we know we should do, until one day we wake up and discover that it is too late.

But what if it wasn't too late after all?...

Mother Knew Best

Raquel was angry!

She was angry at her boyfriend. She was angry at her boss. She was angry at herself. She was angry at the world!

And even though Raquel's parents had both been dead for over five years, she was still angry at them, too! (She had discovered that in the second year of her therapy.)

Raquel lived with her boyfriend Manuel. He had a son from a previous marriage, and Raquel had a daughter, Aurora, and a son, Mike, from previous relationships. So the only way they could make sure someone was always home with the kids was for him to work the day shift and for her to work the night shift. Because of this, they hardly ever saw each other any more, and when they did see each other in passing they were both so tired or pressed for time that they no longer had much of a relationship.

So here she found herself in the middle of the night in the almost-deserted Denver office of "Quik 800 Response," a company that offered answering services for business 800 numbers.

Raquel was currently assigned to take orders for the "Big Bad Black Bear," a teddy bear meant for inner-city kids. But since it was the middle of the night, she got maybe one order an hour, so she actually spent most of her shift either chatting with other bored 800-number order takers around the country or surfing the 'Net.

Tonight she decided to do some surfing, so she logged onto the 'Net to see if there were any interesting chat groups going on. (Sometimes she joined in women's chat groups, and other times she just "listened in" on the sex discussions.)

While scanning the menu, she saw an item that she had never seen before: "Mother Knows Best, a help line for daughters who have lost their way." Intrigued, Raquel typed in the address code and a greeting:

Raquel: Hello, anyone there?

Mother Knows Best: Yes, dear, I'm right here.
What seems to be your problem?

R: Problems, you mean. I hate everything about my life.

MKB: What, for example?

R: Well, for starters, I hate my job. I also hate my boyfriend.

MKB: Why do you hate your boyfriend?

(Raquel had been over this territory with her therapist many times before, so she had practically memorized the answers to these questions.)

R: I guess the real reason I hate him is that he doesn't earn enough money. If he earned more money, then I could quit this stupid job and get a normal life.

MKB: And what would that be?

R: That's the problem. I'd really like to stay home and take care of my kids, but I also feel like I should be working.

MKB: Why is that?

R: I don't know. Maybe because of Women's Lib. I guess I'm afraid that I'd feel guilty and bored taking care of my children all of the time.

MKB: You know, when I was your age, we thought that taking care of our kids was a very important job.

R: How old are you?

MKB: 72.

R: You are the same age that my mom would have been if she was alive.

But just then a call came in from someone in Cleveland who wanted to order the Big Bad Black Bear for her grandchild, so Raquel had to terminate the keyboard conversation.

The next night was also slow, however, so Raquel decided to try to get right back in on the Mother Knows Best line.

R: Hello, are you there?

MKB: Yes, dear.

R: Do you remember me? I was chatting with you last night about the relationship I am in.

MKB: You know, when I was younger, we didn't talk about being "in" a relationship or "in" a marriage.

R: So what did you say?

MKB: Well, we said that we were "going with" someone or that we were "married to" someone, not that we were "in" anything. That sounds like you're "in jail," without any say in the matter.

R: Sometimes being "in" a relationship feels like being in jail.

MKB: And why is that?

R: Because I can't leave.

MKB: Why?

R: Well, for one thing, I don't have enough money to. And, for another thing, Manuel wouldn't let me.

MKB: He wouldn't? I thought you said that you and he aren't getting along.

R: We're not, but he is still very jealous. He's afraid I may be cheating on him or something. He still thinks he owns me.

MKB: It doesn't sound like a very good relationship. Why don't you find someone else?

R: All of the single men I met before I met Manuel were either creeps, queers, bums, druggies, or psychopaths. He was the best of the bunch.

MKB: Where did you go to meet men?

R: Mostly bars.

MKB: Maybe you should have tried looking in other places.

R: You sound like my own mother! It wouldn't have made any difference. The nice guys are all taken and the other ones all seem to be angry at women.

MKB: You sound pretty angry at men, too.

R: You're right.

MKB: I wonder why men and women are so angry at each other these days. When I was younger, we weren't so mad at each other.

R: Why not?

MKB: I think it was because back then we women understood that it is just as hard to be a man as it is to be a woman, but that we were each important in our own way. So we supported and respected each other more and didn't make so many demands on each other. We had all gone through the

Depression and World War II together, so we were grateful for the prosperity in the 'Fifties and the fact that we could raise our kids in peace. The men were grateful to have their jobs and their wives were grateful that their husbands had jobs.

R: Didn't you want to get out of the house and work like your husband did?

MKB: Heavens, no! You see, back then, men and women shared a kind of unspoken understanding.

We women knew that most of them had boring, dirty, dangerous, dead-end or demeaning jobs, but we also knew that they worked at them in order to earn the love and respect of their wives and children and the respect of society in general. So we pretended we were respecting them for what they did at work, and the men pretended to like and be proud of their jobs.

But, in reality, we loved and respected them just for getting up every day and doing it, because they were doing it for us.

R: But didn't you hate having to treat him that way?

MKB: I didn't have to treat him that way. It was my choice to do so. You see, in those days, we didn't expect to be the same as men.

There were "man things" and "woman things," and we felt pride that we could do the "woman things" well, and we felt grateful if we could find a man who could do the "man things" well. We didn't know that we weren't supposed to be satisfied with our lives.

Just then Raquel had to end the chat because a stepfather in Miami called in to order a Big Bad Black Bear for his stepdaughter.

The next night, as soon as she could, Raquel got back on the 'Net to talk on the Mother Knows Best line.

R: Hello. Are you the same person I was talking to last night?

MKB: Of course. How are you, my dear?

R: Fine, thank you. You know, I was thinking about what you were telling me last night.

        Say, my name is Raquel. How shall I call you?

MKB: Why, "Mother," of course.

R: OK, "Mother," I was thinking about what you were saying last night. You know I always hated the way my mother treated my father. She treated him like a servant would treat a master. But I was thinking that maybe she did that for a reason. After all, he worked hard to support our family.

MKB: So?

R: Well, he'd come home dead tired after working at a boring office job all day long, so I guess he needed to have someone show him that his work was appreciated.

MKB: So why would you want to have a life like your father had?

R: I guess I felt that it wasn't enough just to be a "woman." That, since men were superior to women, or at least held superior positions in society, we should all try to be like them.

MKB: Sounds like the Women's Liberation Movement has had the opposite effect than was intended.

R: What do you mean?

172

MKB: Well, it was supposed to help women be better women, not make them feel like imperfect versions of men.

Once again the conversation was interrupted by someone ordering.

But the next night, Raquel jumped right back into the 'Net.

R: Hello, it's me again.

MKB: Hello, Raquel.

R: Say, do you live anywhere near me?
I live in Colorado. I was wondering if I could meet you some time.

MKB: Oh, I'm afraid that wouldn't be possible. I don't travel anymore.

R: Well, anyway, I was thinking about what you said last night. I think men's and women's roles have gotten so mixed up that it's hard to know how to be a good man or good woman anymore.

MKB: Maybe it's enough just to be a good person.

R: I know why women are angry at men, but why do you think men are so angry at women these days?

MKB: Well, think about it. In my time, men basically had five roles: the breadwinner or hunter; the builder or fixer; the hero; the protector; and the leader. The breadwinner or hunter supported the family; the builder built roads, buildings, ships, and so on, or fixed them when they broke; the hero was the cowboy, or athlete, or movie star; the protector was the policeman, the fireman, the soldier; and the leader was the boss, the editor, the politician.

Women also had five roles: wife, mother, teacher, helper, and paramour. But now there's no longer a tacit understanding between men and women. And women have moved into all five roles that men used to have, so men today don't feel so special anymore. It has taken away their self esteem. In other words, their feelings have been hurt but, because they're men, they can't let us know that. In fact, they may not even know it themselves. So they express their hurt through anger.

R: That may be true, but aren't we supposed to have equality now?

MKB: Well, in reality, what "equality" has meant is that women's opportunities have expanded while men haven't gained anything.

R: How's that? Hasn't equality taken some of the pressure off of men?

MKB: No, it has just added to it. Because if they act like "men," they're attacked for it, but if they don't act like "men," women won't have anything to do with them.

And now, with the sexual revolution and all that, the expectations of both men and women have gotten so high that no member of the opposite sex can possibly satisfy them.

Another order came in for the Big Bad Black Bear.

The next night was the last night of Raquel's five-night work week.

R: Hello, "Mother," are you there?

MKB: Hello, Raquel. How are you?

R: I've really learned a lot from you this week. I wish I'd been able to talk to my own mother like I've been able to talk to you.

MKB: And why didn't you?

R: I guess it was a combination of that anger I was telling you about combined with jealousy that my father loved her so much, along with a little teenage rebellion thrown in. But now I realize that she really was a good mother. She wasn't perfect, but she did the best she could based on what she had learned from her own childhood. I just wish I had told her that when she was alive.

MKB: I'm glad to hear that. Very glad.

R: Say, you sure know how to give good motherly advice.

      How'd you get so wise?

MKB: Oh, from a lifetime of experience. Plus, where I live, there are a lot of other women who have had a lot of experience being mothers.

R: Well, because of what I've learned from you this week, I've decided to stop seeing my therapist.

I think she was just making me angrier and crazier. Instead, Manuel has agreed to start going to pre-marriage counseling with me at the church. And I find I'm not so angry anymore. In fact, tomorrow I'm going to go visit my parents' graves.

MKB: That is good news, isn't it!

R: Well, I won't be here the next two nights, but I'm looking forward to talking to you again next week.

MKB: Unfortunately, I'm afraid that won't be possible. You see, where I live, it is kind of a privilege to give advice through "Mother Knows Best."

In fact, there's a five-year waiting list.

Next week another mother will be here.

R: That's too bad. I'll miss you.

Well, thanks, "Mother," for all of your advice. It's too bad you weren't able to be here longer.

MKB: I agree, I agree. Well, good-bye, Raquel.

I hope we can talk again someday, maybe in five years. And please give my love to Mike and Aurora, and tell them how much I miss them.

The End

The Gift of the Magic

Richard Showstack is a full-time writer in Southern California. If you would like to get in touch with him, please send your e-mail to: Fables4Teenagers@AOL.com

Books from Science & Humanities Press

Me and My Shadows — Shadow Puppet Fun for Kids of All Ages - Elizabeth Adams, Revised Edition by Dr. Bud Banis (2000) A thoroughly illustrated guide to the art of shadow puppet entertainment using tools that are always at hand wherever you go. A perfect gift for children and adults. ISBN 1-888725-44-3, 7X8¼, 67 pp, 12.95

MamaSquad! (2001) Hilarious novel by Clarence Wall about what happens when a group of women from a retirement home get tangled up in Army Special Forces. ISBN 1-888725-13-3 5½ X8¼, 200 pp, $14.95

Virginia Mayo — The Best Years of My Life (2002) Autobiography of film star Virginia Mayo as told to LC Van Savage. From her early days in Vaudeville and the Muny in St Louis to the dozens of hit motion pictures, with dozens of photographs. ISBN 1-888725-53-2, 5½ X 8¼, 200 pp, $18.95

The Job — Eric Whitfield (2001) A story of self-discovery in the context of the death of a grandfather. A book to read and share in times of change and Grieving. ISBN 1-888725-68-0, 5½ X 8¼, 100 pp, $14.95

To Norma Jeane With Love, Jimmie -Jim Dougherty as told to LC Van Savage (2001) ISBN 1-888725-51-6 The sensitive and touching story of Jim Dougherty's teenage bride who later became Marilyn Monroe. Dozens of photographs. "The Marilyn Monroe book of the year!" As seen on TV. 5½X8¼, 200 pp, $16.95

Riverdale Chronicles — Charles F. Rechlin (2003). Life, living and character studies in the setting of the Riverdale Golf Club by Charles F. Rechlin 5½ X 8¼, 100 pp ISBN: 1-888725-84-2 $14.95

Books by Richard Showstack

The Gift of the Magic -and other enchanting character-building stories for smart teenage girls who want to grow up to be strong women. Richard Showstack, (2004) 1-888725-64-8 5½ X8¼, 145 pp, $14.95

A Horse Named Peggy-and other enchanting character-building stories for smart teenage boys who want to grow up to be good men. Richard Showstack, (2004) 1-888725-66-4. 5½ X8¼, 145 pp, $14.95

Order Form			
Item	Each	Quantity	Amount
Missouri (only) sales tax 6.925%			
Priority Shipping			$5.00
	Total		

BeachHouse Books
PO Box 7151
 Chesterfield, MO 63006-7151
(636) 394-4950

www.beachhousebooks.com